THE PEANUTS MOVIE

by Schulz

Charlie Brown Is Not a Quitter!

based on the *Peanuts* comic strip by Charles M. Schulz
adapted by Maggie Testa

Simon Spotlight

New York London Toronto Sydney New Delhi

SIMON SPOTLIGHT

An imprint of Simon & Schuster Children's Publishing Division

1230 Avenue of the Americas, New York, New York 10020

This Simon Spotlight hardcover edition September 2015

For information about special discounts for bulk purchases, please contact Simon & Schuster

Charlie Brown felt ready. Charlie Brown felt determined. Charlie Brown felt a perfect breeze in the air. "This could be the day!" he announced.

What was Charlie Brown hoping to do?

Fly his kite once and for all!

At first, it looked like Charlie Brown would succeed. As he ran through the snow, his kite got higher and higher until . . .

. . . he slipped on the ice and the kite started pulling *him* along. Charlie Brown got caught in a hockey net, then knocked into Lucy and ruined her famous Triple Axel. Worst of all, the kite was gobbled up by a tree, leaving Charlie Brown dangling upside down!

"What kind of person tries to fly a kite in the middle of winter?" said Lucy angrily. "You'll never achieve any success. Why? Because you're Charlie Brown."

Linus helped him down from the tree, and Charlie Brown wandered over to the baseball diamond. Maybe today wouldn't be the day he finally flew a kite, but it could be the day he perfected his pitching!

"I don't care what Lucy says," Charlie Brown muttered to himself. "I may have had troubles in the past flying a kite, and I may never have won a baseball game, but it's not for lack of trying. My pitching *has* to improve if I come out to my trusty mound every day. Charlie Brown is not a quitter!"

"Let's see if you can handle my fastball," Charlie Brown said, throwing a snowball to home plate.

Whack! Apparently the snowman hitter had no problem handling Charlie Brown's fastball!

"It's going to be a long winter," moaned Charlie Brown.

But Charlie Brown didn't have time to feel sorry for himself. A stampede of kids was gathering at the fence. Something was happening!

Charlie Brown saw a moving truck pull to a stop in front of his house. "Someone's moving in across the street from me," he said in awe.

Whoever it is, he thought, *he or she would know nothing of my past imperfections. This could be my chance to start over with a clean slate.*

As Charlie Brown daydreamed, he leaned a little too hard on the fence . . . and it fell down into the snow.

"*He* did it!" all the kids cried.

Maybe my fresh start can begin tomorrow, thought Charlie Brown.

The next day at school, Charlie Brown and his classmates met the new kid. It was a girl—a little red-haired girl.

Charlie Brown's face turned bright red and his knees felt weak. He couldn't stop his heart from beating really fast, he couldn't stop smiling, and he certainly couldn't concentrate on the big test he was supposed to be taking.

At the last minute, he filled in random answers and hurried up to the teacher's desk to hand in his test. Charlie Brown knew he should be worried about his score, but he was too excited to meet the new girl to care!

When he got home from school, Charlie Brown rushed upstairs and looked out the window at the house across the street. He wanted to go over and talk to the Little Red-Haired Girl, but he didn't have the nerve.

"What are you looking at, big brother?" asked Sally, opening the blinds.

"Are you crazy?" cried Charlie Brown.

Sally understood. "Oh, you like her!" she remarked.

Somehow, later that day, Charlie Brown found the courage to walk over to the Little Red-Haired Girl's house. Snoopy came with him.

Charlie Brown was pleased that Snoopy was by his side. "It's times like this that you need your faithful friend," he told Snoopy.

But just as Charlie Brown was about to ring the doorbell . . . he lost his nerve and started walking away. Snoopy had to push Charlie Brown back in the right direction.

Charlie Brown went to ring the doorbell for a second time, but he still couldn't bring himself to do it. So Snoopy did it for him!

The front door opened. "Hello?" said the Little Red-Haired Girl. She didn't see anyone, so she went back inside.

Poor Charlie Brown!

Charlie Brown needed advice, so he headed to Lucy's booth.

"What brings you here so late in the day?" Lucy asked him.

"I need your advice on girls," he replied. Then he told her how hard it was for him to find the courage to talk to the Little Red-Haired Girl.

Lucy knew just what Charlie Brown needed to hear. "Girls want winners," she told him.

THE DOCTOR

"Lucy, you may be on to something!" exclaimed Charlie Brown.

"Of course, I don't mean you," Lucy explained. "You know you couldn't possibly win anything. That'll be five cents, please."

Charlie Brown paid Lucy her nickel, but he didn't pay attention to the last part of what she said. He knew what he needed to do. He needed to find a way to impress the Little Red-Haired Girl and become a winner!

And he knew just the place to do it—at the talent show! Charlie Brown decided to perform a magic act. He practiced until every detail was perfect. For his big finale, he would pull Snoopy out of his hat, and then Snoopy would pull Woodstock out of his hat. Ta-da!

"I have a really good feeling tonight is the night I'm going to wow her," Charlie Brown said confidently on the night of the show.

Sally went on before Charlie Brown, but her little rodeo act was a disaster! So Charlie Brown took off his magician's costume, went onstage, and rescued his little sister . . . only to end up being lassoed by her!

The audience burst into laughter.

The next day at school, everyone was talking about Charlie Brown's performance in Sally's act. But that wasn't the only thing they were talking about: The winter dance was coming up.

That afternoon, Charlie Brown saw the Little Red-Haired Girl practicing her dance moves through her front window. That gave him another idea for how to become a winner. He could show her what a great dancer he was.

But first he had to actually learn how to dance. Once again, it was Snoopy to the rescue!

By the night of the dance, Charlie Brown was ready. He entered the dance competition. The girls went first and the Little Red-Haired Girl won! She would dance with the winner for the boys. Would it be Charlie Brown?

Charlie Brown's chances were looking good! His moves were a little out there, but everyone cheered him on.

"It's going to happen," Charlie Brown whispered to himself. "I'm about to dance with the Little Red-Haired Girl!"

But then Charlie Brown kicked his foot up in the air and his shoe went flying. It hit the sprinkler, which went off and sent everyone running out of the gym—including the Little Red-Haired Girl.

"This isn't how it was supposed to end," Charlie Brown said, putting his shoe

Charlie Brown was sure that once again everyone would be talking about him at school the next day. And they were, but not because of what happened at the dance. Someone got a perfect score on the big test—and it was Charlie Brown!

All of a sudden, kids couldn't get enough of Charlie Brown. They loved his artwork! They wanted his advice! They picked him for their hockey teams!

Sally even started giving tours of their home.

"This is his bed, where he lies and ponders life's greatest questions," she explained as she led her tour group through Charlie Brown's room.

Charlie Brown was definitely on his way to becoming a winner!

To top it off, there was an assembly to celebrate Charlie Brown's achievement.

"It's finally going to happen," Charlie Brown told Linus. "The Little Red-Haired Girl is going to notice me for something great."

Charlie Brown ran up to take his place onstage as the guest of honor.

"Today is declared Charlie Brown Day," announced Marcie. "Here is your test to keep as a memento."

It was the proudest moment of Charlie Brown's life—until he looked down at the test. These weren't his answers! There must have been a mix-up. Charlie Brown knew what he had to do.

"Thank you all for your support," he began, "but there's been a mistake. This is not my test. Therefore I cannot accept this honor."

Charlie Brown walked offstage. He had never felt more like quitting. But what he didn't know was that someone had been watching him do the right thing again and again.

The Little Red-Haired Girl told Charlie Brown how much she admired him. "You showed compassion for your sister at the talent show, honesty at the assembly, and at the dance, you were brave and funny."

Charlie Brown couldn't stop smiling—the fact that he didn't give up was the reason the Little Red-Haired Girl wanted to be his friend!

"It must feel pretty great being Charlie Brown right about now," said Linus.

"I'm proud to be your little sister, big brother," Sally chimed in.

"This time you've really gone and done it, you blockhead," said Lucy. Then she smiled. "You've shown me a whole new side of yourself. Good ol' Charlie Brown!"